# Magnificent Mermaids

## COLORING BOOK

### MARJORIE SARNAT

**DOVER PUBLICATIONS, INC.**
MINEOLA, NEW YORK

Inside this stunning coloring book, you will find the magical underwater world of mermaids! Mermaids are beloved for their legendary beauty and are known as spirits of love and friendship. This book contains 31 images of these delightful mythological creatures swimming with dolphins, riding a giant sea turtle, playing a flute, and posing with an underwater treasure chest. Specially designed for experienced colorists, Creative Haven® coloring books offer an escape to a world of inspiration and artistic fulfillment, and perforated pages printed on one side only make displaying your finished artwork easy.

*Bibliographical Note*

*Magnificent Mermaids Coloring Book* is a new work,
first published by Dover Publications, Inc., in 2019.

*International Standard Book Number*
*ISBN-13: 978-0-486-83251-7*
*ISBN-10: 0-486-83251-1*

Manufactured in the United States by LSC Communications
83251105    2020
www.doverpublications.com